Disney's DUCKTALES

Scrooge McDuck
and the Big Surprise

By Cindy West

Illustrated by

Bill Langley and Diana Wakeman

A Golden Book • New York

Western Publishing Company, Inc., Racine, Wisconsin 53404

Scrooge McDuck got a letter.
"Who sent me this letter?"
he said.
Huey, Dewey, and Louie
just smiled.

The letter said,
"Take the train to
a big surprise."
"Money!" thought Scrooge.
That was the surprise
he liked best.
"Come on, boys!" he said.

"Look at that truck!"
cried Huey.
"So what?"
said Scrooge.
"That is not
the big surprise.
I will know it
when I see it."

"Look at that pony!"
cried Dewey.
"So what?"
said Scrooge.
"That is not
the big surprise."

"Look at all that corn!"
cried Louie.
"So what?"
said Scrooge.
"That is not
the big surprise."

Scrooge got another letter.
"Who sent me THIS letter?"
he said.
Huey, Dewey, and Louie
just smiled.

The letter said,
"Take the boat to
a big surprise."
Scrooge and the boys
got on the boat.

"Look at that ball!"
cried Huey.
"So what?"
said Scrooge.
"That is not
the big surprise."

"Look at all those fish!"
cried Dewey.
"So what?"
said Scrooge.
"That is not
the big surprise.
I will know it
when I see it."

"Look up!"
cried Louie.
Scrooge looked up.
He saw an airplane.

The airplane made
words in the sky.
The words said,
"Follow me to
a big surprise."

"How can I follow
that airplane?"
said Scrooge.
Huey, Dewey, and Louie
just smiled.

Just then
Launchpad McQuack
came by.
"Come with me,"
he said.

"Look at that balloon!"
cried Huey.
"So what?"
said Scrooge.
"That is not
the big surprise.
I will know it
when I see it."

Soon the airplane landed.
Launchpad landed by
the airplane.
"Where are we?"
said Scrooge.
"Where is the big surprise?"

Scrooge looked around.
"Look at all these pennies!"
he said.
"They are just pennies.
But this is more like
a big surprise now."

Scrooge saw some words.
The words said,
"Follow the pennies to
a big surprise."

"Come on, boys!" said Scrooge.
"We will find
the big surprise.
We will find
the money."
Huey, Dewey, and Louie
just smiled.

Scrooge ran and ran.

He saw a tent.

He saw all his friends.

He saw some words.

The words said,

"HAPPY BIRTHDAY, SCROOGE!"

"Well, well," said Scrooge.
"This is not what I had thought.
But I know a big surprise
when I see one."
"Surprise!" yelled Huey, Dewey,
and Louie.

"I am happy,"
said Scrooge.
"A party with friends
is the *best* big surprise
of all!"